IS THAT YOUR DOG?

A Mammoth Read

mammoth

by

STEVE MAY

Steve

If you enjoyed reading this book, you might also like to try another story from the **<u>Mammoth Read</u>** series:

pictures
by

WOODROW
PHOENIX

For S M M,
Better late than never
SM

Walkies: Bonnie, Science, Hawkins, Bobby, Diva,
Tolstoy & Tanya, Ben, Sheba, Paddy, Patch,
Nutmeg & Shady, Muffin, Clarry,
Amy . . . and Corinne
WP

First published in Great Britain in 2001
by Mammoth, an imprint of Egmont Children's Books Limited
a division of Egmont Holding Limited
239 Kensington High Street, London, W8 6SA

Text copyright © 2001 Steve May
Illustrations copyright © 2001 Woodrow Phoenix

The moral rights of the author and illustrator have been asserted.

ISBN 0 7497 4247 X

3 5 7 9 10 8 6 4 2

A CIP catalogue record for this book
is available from the British Library

Printed in Great Britain by Cox & Wyman, Ltd
Reading, Berkshire

Contents

'My pet is a dog. His name is Bucket. He's naughty but very friendly if he likes you. . .'

1. Liar!

'Liar!'

'Liar!'

'Liar!'

The three girls glared at Jim.

Jim said, 'But it's true, honest,
I have got a dog.'

'What's his name, then?' demanded Sarah.

'What's he look like?' demanded Anna.

'How big is he?' demanded Jane.

Jim explained: 'His name's Bucket, he's three years old, he's a wire-haired terrier.'

'Huh,' said Sarah.

'Huh,' said Anna.

'Huh,' said Jane.

'I'll show you, I'll prove it,' said Jim. And he pushed past the girls and walked on home.

When he got home, the house was quiet. His mum was in her study, working. It was a big house, with wooden floors and things that needed doing. Jim clomped up the stairs. His feet made big, empty noises on

the bare boards.

'Can you keep the noise down?' his mum called.

'Sure,' Jim whispered.

'What?' shouted his mum.

'Sure!!!'

His mum looked out from her study.

'There's no need to shout.'

Jim picked up the telephone on the landing.

'Hi, Bill, it's Jim.'

Bill is Jim's cousin.

'What do you want this time?' Bill asked.

Jim said, 'I just want to come over and hang out.

'OK,' said Bill, 'if you must, but I'm going out at six.'

Jim ran all the way to Bill's house.

2. Bucket

Bill's house was big, with a big garden.

Jim ran down the path beside the house.

'Woof, woof, woof, woof!'

Barring his way is a dog. A wire-haired terrier, with flashing eyes. The dog doesn't look friendly.

'Hi, Bucket,' Jim said.

The dog didn't reply.

Except, it growled.

Jim hesitated. 'Bucket, you know me,' he said.

The dog shook its head.

'Come on, Jim, what's holding you back?'

That's Bill, shouting from the back garden.

Jim edged past Bucket the dog.

'You've got to show a dog you're not scared of it,' Bill said.

'I'm not scared, I'm just cautious,' Jim said.

Bill was sat on the ground. Bucket was sat between his legs, bristling under his wiry brows. Watching every little movement in the garden.

Bill picked up a rubber ring.

Immediately, Bucket went on red alert. He bounced round on to all four paws, with his bum sticking out backwards and his head near the ground.

Bill waved the rubber ring around.

Bucket was growling and barking and yapping and jumping up at Bill. Bill playfully fended off the dog. Bucket was trying to grab the ring with his mouth.

'Can I have a go?' Jim asked.

'Sure.'

Bill tossed him the ring.

Bucket changed course in midair, and snapped.

Jim, reaching out with his hand, reached back quickly.

Bucket caught the ring SNAP in his mouth and backed away, wagging his stumpy tail.

'You'll never get it back now,' Bill said.

Jim advanced, Bucket backed off.

Jim grabbed at the ring, Bucket darted backwards, still in reverse.

Jim ran, Bucket ran too.

Bucket ran round and round the garden. He slowed down, Jim got closer, then Bucket speeded up again.

Finally, Jim cornered Bucket by the shed. Bucket dropped the ring between his front paws, and glared up at Jim, and bristled.

Jim reached down to pick up the ring. Bucket barked, and leaped up and snapped at the air centimetres from Jim's fingers.

Jim went back and sat by Bill.

Bill laughed.

On the grass was some of Bucket's wiry fur.

When Bill wasn't looking, Jim picked it up and put it in his pocket.

It's just a matter of experience, Jim told himself. If I had a dog, I'd know how to handle a dog.

On his way home, he called in at the pet shop. He bought a lead and a book about dogs.

That evening, Jim went strolling through the

park. He had the lead in one hand and a stick in the other. He passed the swing park. Sarah and Anna and Jane were there. They ran to the fence.

'What are you doing?'

'Walking my dog.'

'Where is he?'

Jim pointed towards the woods. 'Chasing rabbits.'

'Huh,' said Sarah.

'Huh,' said Anna.

'Huh,' said Jane.

Jim strolled towards the woods.

The three girls followed him.

There was the sound of barking from deep within the woods.

'There he is,' Jim said.

The girls frowned.

Jim slapped the lead against his leg and called, 'Bucket! Bucket!'

And he strode off into the woods.

3. No turning back

Next day in school, the girls were talking about Jim and his dog.

'We never saw it.'

'I think he's making it up.'

'Yeah?' said Tariq. 'Then why did he come in our shop and buy five tins of dog food?'

'And look at all the doggy

hair all over his jumper,' said Ben. 'It's disgusting.'

Jim studied his dog book carefully. He learned all he could about dog health and training and grooming. That week, in his school diary, he wrote a long essay about dogs in general, and his dog in particular. Mrs Croft gave him a red star.

'If your dog's so real,' said Sarah, 'why don't you enter him for the school Fun Charity Pet Show?'

Jim went cold inside. He said, 'Sure, I will.'

Next day, in assembly, Mrs Andrews reminded everyone, 'The Fun Charity Pet Show is tomorrow. Closing date for entries is this afternoon.'

Good, thought Jim. I'll be too late.

But that afternoon, the girls found him after

school, and surrounded him.

'Have you done your entry yet?'

'Not quite.'

'Why not?'

Jim thought quickly, 'They ran out of forms.'

'That's OK,' said Sarah, 'we brought you one.'

And they sat Jim down, and made him fill it in.

When he'd filled it in, they made him take it to Mrs Andrews' office, and post it in the entry box.

Plop.

Gone.

No turning back.

Jim went home.

His mum was making a sandwich. 'I've been thinking,' she said, 'about getting a pet.'

Jim's heart flew up in his chest like a bird.

'I need a dog!'

'You *want*, don't *need*,' she said, slapping the sandwich together, 'but at the moment we can't cope with a dog . . .'

'It's me, not we . . .'

'So I thought maybe we could start off with a gerbil or something small.'

Jim shook his head, turned, and walked away.

'Or even a guinea-pig!' his mum called

after him.

But Jim had gone.

He sat in his bedroom, but there wasn't much space, what with all the tins of dog food. So, he got his lead, and his stick, and went for a walk.

He walked through the park.

Lots of people out with dogs. Big dogs, small dogs, slow dogs, fast dogs. So many dogs in the world, and he didn't have one. Was it too much to ask? For there to be a sort

of mistake, so at the end of the day he had one, and someone else didn't?

People nodded to him, said hello.

He said hello back.

He threw his stick.

He called his dog.

All the time he was thinking.

He had to get a dog from somewhere. By tomorrow.

4. I need your dog

Bill said, 'What?'

Jim said, 'I need to borrow your dog.'

'What for?'

Jim thought quickly.

'There's a poor old woman down our road, and she's very ill, and she loves dogs, but she's too old and sick to have one, and the doctor said it would cheer her up if someone brought a dog round to visit.'

Bill shook his head.

Bucket, sitting in front of them, shook his head too.

'It's true!' pleaded Jim.

'OK,' said Bill, 'let's go now.'

'No, no, no, not now!'

Bill sat down again. 'Why not?'

'Because,' said Jim, 'old Mrs Hubbard . . .'

'Mrs Hubbard?'

'That's her name. She's so poorly she's in hospital until . . . until tomorrow morning.'

'OK,' said Bill, 'tomorrow it is. We'll go then.'

'The thing is,' Jim said, 'she's

very frail and she scares easily and she doesn't like strangers so really it's best if I go on my own.'

Bucket yapped.

Bill said, 'If she scares easily, she's not going to like Bucket, is she?'

'It's different with dogs. She's used to dogs. She used to be in a circus and make them run round with carts tied to them.'

As soon as he said it, Jim knew he'd said the wrong thing.

Bucket yelped loudly, and shuddered.

Bill shook his head. 'No way,' he said, 'no way does Bucket get involved with circus kind of things.'

'But she's very kind, she looks after her dogs, there's pictures of her meeting the Queen . . .'

Bucket shuddered again.

It was no use.

'And anyway,' said Bill, 'we're going away this weekend. So there's no way we could help you, even if we wanted to.'

Bill got up and walked back towards his house.

Bucket got up and trotted just behind him. Alert, loyal, wiry with mischief.

Walking home, Jim passed the usual shops. He didn't pay much attention. Until one caught his eye: THE DOG PROTECTION LEAGUE.

It was a charity sort of place. The window crammed with old tat. Jim went in. There was more tat inside, and a smell like wet blankets drying out, and a young woman.

She was sitting behind the old-fashioned till, sewing up an ancient pair of trousers.

'I need a dog,' Jim said.

The young woman looked at him. 'We don't sell dogs,' she said, 'we protect them.'

'Where are they, then?' demanded Jim, peering round the shop.

'They're in our dogs' home.'

'Where's that?'

The woman reached under her counter and fetched out a leaflet.

'Thanks,' said Jim, and headed for the door.

'It's a serious business,' the woman called after him.

'I know that,' Jim said.

On the way to the dogs' home he read the

leaflet. It said that thousands of people every year bought dogs and then found they didn't want them.

Crazy! Can you believe that?

And then they take the dog out in the car miles from home and leave it on the motorway.

Jim heard the dogs' home before he saw it.

In the distance, a faint yapping in the air, woofing and barking and howling. As he got closer, the noises got louder. It was like a mad choir, with all sorts of doggy voices: high and deep and loud and yappy.

They all sounded sad.

Jim rang the bell.

'What can I do for you?' the woman asked.

'I hear you've got some dogs.'

'That's right,' she replied. 'Do you want to come and see them?'

'Yes please.'

So the woman let him in, and showed him round the dogs' home. The dogs were kept in individual cages. The cages weren't very big.

'We'd like them to be bigger,' the woman explained, 'but it's a matter of space. And there's so many dogs we have to look after.'

There were all sorts of dogs in the cages. Most of them barked and howled. Some of them just sat, or lay, with sad eyes. They all stared at Jim as he passed.

'The thing is,' Jim said, 'I want to help out.'

'That's good,' nodded the woman.

'I thought maybe I could take a dog for a walk.'

'When?'

'Tomorrow.'

The woman frowned. 'They're not toys, you know.'

'I know that.'

'We like to get to know our volunteers, and get them to do a variety of jobs . . .'

'OK, OK,' said Jim, 'if I do all that, can I take a dog for a walk tomorrow afternoon between three and five?'

The woman looked at him. 'No,' she said. 'We'd have to get to know you for at least a week. And we'd need to talk to your parents.'

'That wouldn't help,' said Jim.

5.
Desperation,
Plan Z

Jim couldn't sleep that night.

Every time he nearly fell asleep, he heard a yappy bark, and three girls laughing. Then he woke up, hot and sweating, with a funny feeling in his chest, as if he'd lost something valuable. In the morning, he felt sick, couldn't eat.

'What's up?' asked his mum.

'Nothing.'

'I thought we could go to the pet show this afternoon.'

'No way.'

'But if you're so keen on animals . . .'

'I can't. I've got footie practice.'

There was only one chance now. Plan Z. Desperation.

Jim marched up the road, and knocked on the door of number seventy-six. He waited, then knocked again. And again, and again.

He edged round the concrete front garden, and peered in the window.

Through the creamy net curtains he could see her. Mrs Jotham. In front of the blaring television. And next to Mrs Jotham, Lively.

Jim banged on the window. He put his hands to his mouth, and called. He went back to the front door, and bent down, and forced the narrow letterbox open, and put his mouth right up to the metal, and shouted.

'Mrs Jotham!'

The door opened.
Mrs Jotham stood there,
peering this way and that.

'Hello, my dear, where are you?'

'Here, Mrs Jotham. It's Jim from up the road.'

'Long time no see,' replied the old lady.

Then Lively arrived. Better late than never. Lively was a poodle, once white, now faded grey. He rushed to the front door, yapping. His rush was now more of a stumble, slipping on the lino. He couldn't get his legs going in the right order. But his yap was still loud and short and scary. When he stopped yapping, his breath came in gasps, and he growled in his throat.

His eyes were like pearl buttons. Glazed over. He glanced this way, that way, up and down. He must be almost totally blind.

Like his mistress.

'I wondered if Lively wanted a walk,' Jim said.

'I'll ask him,' said Mrs Jotham.

The walk started slowly. Lively paused by the front gate. Mrs Jotham stood hunched in the window, waving. Lively sniffed the fresh air, and then slowly started to turn round.

'No you don't,' hissed Jim, and yanked on the lead.

'Gggggggggggg,' choked Lively.

Jim pulled him along the street.

They passed a poster advertising the school Fun Charity Pet Show.

OK, so Lively is an old grey poodle called Lively, not a wire-haired terrier called Bucket, but at least he's a dog.

Lively's legs were moving, but they couldn't get a grip. He was sliding.

At the corner of the street, Jim stopped. It was another half a mile to the school. He looked down at the dog. Lively was shivering,

gasping, coughing. Never going to make it.
Jim bent over and touched the dog's head.
The fur felt slick, slimy. Lively looked up, eyes
like buttons. Peering.

'It's OK, boy,' Jim said. And reached down
slowly, till both his hands were a few
centimetres away from the dog's grey,
greasy fur.

'Do it!' Jim urged himself. And clasped.

He could feel Lively's mess of bones under
the slimy fur.

Jim lifted.

Lively wheezed and croaked. Still peering,
the dog stuck out his tongue, urged his head
forward, and licked Jim's cheek.

The dog's breath smelled like dog food,
with some sewage mixed in. The wet patch on
Jim's cheek felt as though it was hardening

over, like glue.

A fly buzzed past, turned, and zoomed in, interested.

Jim turned and walked back along the road towards number seventy-six.

He was still carrying the dog.

There was no need to ring on the bell. Mrs Jotham was waiting.

'I was watching out the window,' she said.

'We had a lovely walk,' Jim said.

'Good,' said Mrs Jotham.

6. Blast!

Jim wandered down the street. He'd had it. No dog, no show. Maybe he ought to go to a motorway somewhere and wait for bad people to abandon a puppy. But it wasn't Christmas, was it?

'RAAAAAWF!!!'

Jim's heart shot up his throat like a jumping fish.

He turned to see what made the noise.

There, tied to a lamppost with a dirty old piece of string, was a dog.

A huge dog.

A fat black dog with dark eyes and a droopy mouth.

His tail was wagging.

'RAAAAAWF!' The dog barked again, then

looked round, as if he was embarrassed.

Jim edged up towards the dog.

The dog stared at him out of his black droopy eyes.

There was a tag round the dog's neck. Jim reached out towards the tag.

The dog watched Jim's hand approaching.

The dog looked puzzled, as though he didn't know what a hand was.

Then, when Jim's hand got to within a couple of centimetres of the dog's face, the dog jerked his head back and let out another loud 'RAAAAAWF!'

Jim snatched his hand back.

The dog edged

away a couple of paws, and settled again. Looking shame-faced.

'It's OK, don't be scared,' said Jim. Who was terrified. 'I won't hurt you.'

The thing is, he remembered, to be confident. Don't show you're nervous.

So, he took a step closer to the dog, and reached out his hand again. Not fast, but confident.

The dog's head sank, as though he were expecting a blow. He watched from under his eyebrows.

Jim got hold of the tag, and turned it over.

It was a cheap metal tag, with a piece of card slotted into it. On the card was written one word, in rough ballpoint handwriting: *Blast.*

'Blast?' said Jim.

The dog looked up at him.

'Is that your name? Blast?'

The dog's head nodded, and he shifted on his big paws.

Jim's mind was racing. What to do?

'Is that your dog?' It was a woman come out of the shop.

Jim didn't know what to say. He said, 'I suppose I'm sort of looking after him.'

'Well,' she said, 'he's been out there over an hour. I think it's a disgrace.'

And she huffed back into the shop.

Aha! So, maybe he's been abandoned. Or lost? So the best thing to do, is take him to the dogs' home. Then if he belongs to someone they can claim him. And meanwhile, if Jim happens to call in at the school, where there happens to be a pet show, what of it?

At that moment, Blast let out another 'RAAAAWF!' and stood up, and wriggled his head. He was staring across the road.

Across the road was a cat. A neat little black and white cat, padding along the pavement, minding its own business.

Blast's eyes widened, and he shook himself, and he took off.

Forget the string, forget the road. The string ripped and the cars honked, and Blast was away.

TOOOT

SCREEECH

BEEBEEEP

BEEP

HONK

PAARP

BEEEP

The cat heard him, and turned. For a
moment the cat kept up his cool. Then,
when he saw what was coming,
he took off, too. Cool
no more.

HONK

HONNNK

He shot
down the
street. Blast charged
after the cat, and Jim chased
after Blast. The cat swerved and
slithered through a gap in the fence.
Blast reached the fence, and stood, panting,
staring at the hole.

'I think he got away,' Jim said.

Blast glanced up at him, and then glared
back at the hole in the fence.

'I don't think he's coming back,' Jim said.

Blast didn't answer. He sat down, staring patiently at the hole.

Jim clipped his lead on to Blast's collar. Blast paid no attention. He was too interested in the hole in the fence.

'Come on,' said Jim, 'we'll come back later.'

7. Adverts

Blast was a slow walker. He walked like an old man with no sandals on a pebbly beach. Picking his way. He didn't seem to mind the lead. He walked with his head hanging, and his face drooping. Jim's head was high. He felt proud. Ahead, there was a woman with an Alsatian.

Blast's miles better than him, Jim thought.

The Alsatian eyed Blast. Blast paid no attention. He picked his way along, as though the pavement was red-hot, with his head hanging, and his face frowning.

The woman saw Blast, and pulled the Alsatian's lead, so he was choked back.

The Alsatian, eyes wide, started doing little lunging movements with its head.

'Good afternoon,' said the woman.

'Nice day,' said Jim.

The Alsatian flung itself at Blast, pulling the woman with it. She clung on. Blast stopped walking, and stared at the Alsatian, which was now snapping and yapping a couple of centimetres from him.

Blast looked puzzled, as though he couldn't quite work out what this yapping, snapping, spittley thing was.

The Alsatian made another, stronger lunge, and pulled the woman, and snapped at Blast's shoulder.

Blast shrugged the shoulder, and walked on.

The Alsatian lunged and plunged and snapped and yapped.

The woman dug her heels in, and clung on to the Alsatian's lead.

'He's never usually like this,' she said.

'Good boy,' Jim said to Blast.

Blast glanced up at Jim, and carried on walking.

It was the same with every dog they met. Big dogs, little dogs, poodles, terriers, mongrels, retrievers – as soon as they saw Blast, they wanted to have a fight. But Blast wasn't interested.

They came to the department store. In the window were twelve televisions, all showing the same programme.

Jim stopped to have a look, and Blast sat down and watched too. It was football, and only two minutes to go to half-time. United were one up. Jim watched. Blast sat, patiently waiting.

The half ended.

'Come on,' said Jim.

But Blast was watching the adverts. The first advert was for cat food.

Blast's face woke up. The droopy bits stretched out. He stood up, and pressed his face closer to the glass. On all twelve TV sets, a fat, spoiled cat was walking towards its bowl of food.

Blast's eyes flickered here and there, here and there, trying to keep up with all these cats at once.

'Raaaaawf!'

It wasn't a very loud raaawf, because he couldn't lift his head, because if he lifted his

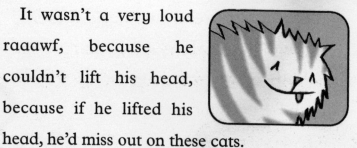

head, he'd miss out on these cats.

All twelve cats were now crouched down, licking at their bowls.

This was too much for Blast.

He lunged.

The lunge took Jim by surprise. Blast thudded into the glass, head first. He drew back, and lunged again. Another thud.

Jim tried to keep hold of the lead.

Blast lunged a third time. Harder. The glass shook.

'They're not real cats,' Jim said. 'They're inside, on TV.'

Blast looked up at him, puzzled.

'In the shop,' Jim explained again, pointing.

'Raaaawf!' exclaimed Blast, and he was away, into the department store.

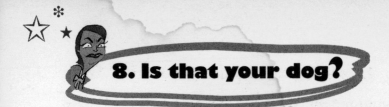

8. Is that your dog?

The department nearest the entrance was the Perfumery. Blast knew there were twelve cats in there somewhere. Probably hiding. He bounded from counter to counter, leaping first one way, then another, jumping up with his front paws to have a look on top. His loose lead flapped and slapped on the glass.

Behind one counter, the fragile woman in her plastered make-up shrank back, with her hand at her throat.

Blast saw what he wanted. He slithered with his front paws on the glass counter, trying to get a grip. His back legs pedalled furiously. He strained his neck forward. His tongue lolled. He let out a high, strangulated 'RAAAAAAWF!'

He got a grip, his back paws batted at the counter, he slithered up and forward like a torpedo, then over the other side.

The woman shrank back.

'He's going to kill me!'

Blast ignored her. He went straight for the cat, hiding in a box behind the woman. He stuck his head into the box, and snapped with his big jaws, and wrenched the cat out. It was soft in his mouth. He shook it and shook it. It smelled like peaches. It was full of sweet-smelling dust and powder.

He sneezed, and
dropped the cat
on the floor,
and stood
over it,
glaring down.

The cat lay on the floor without moving.

It was pink. It had no head, no tail, no legs.

'He's eating my powder puff,' the anxious powdered woman shrilled.

Jim arrived at the counter. 'Blast!' he said.

But Blast, realising his mistake, was away.

'Is that your dog?' the woman asked Jim.

'Sort of,' he said. And set off after Blast.

Blast chased down a wig, but as soon as he got it in his mouth he knew it wasn't a cat, so he bounded out of the Perfumery and headed up the escalator to the Fashion department. It took him a little while to get up there, because he was going up on the down escalator. But he was determined, and he kept bounding and panting, and got there in the end.

At the top of the escalator, he glared around him. Why are cats always so smart? He saw one hiding up a tree thing. The tree was metal, and when Blast stood up and rested his paws on it, the tree fell over and the cat fell out. But as soon as it hit the floor it turned into a slack baggy thing.

Blast tossed the baggy thing in his mouth. Irritated. This was of no interest whatsoever.

A smart woman ran over to him and pulled the baggy thing away.

'He's attacking our hats!' she cried.

Jim puffed up.

Blast bounded away.

'Is that your dog?'

the woman demanded.

'Sort of,' said Jim, following Blast. 'I'm just looking after him.'

'Well,' the woman shouted, 'you're not doing much of a job!'

Jim followed Blast through the Food Hall. Blast hardly paused there. He knew the difference between cooked meat and cats. The German salami fooled him for a moment, because it had a tail of string. But, as soon as he got it in his mouth, Blast tasted the garlic and dropped it on the floor.

Jim got there seconds later, and he might have caught up with Blast except the Food manager got in his way. Waving the salami.

'Is that your dog?'

'No.' And Jim pulled away.

The Food manager waved the salami again.

'Have you any idea how much this is worth?'

'Not much now,' Jim shouted back.

9. Shoot him!

Blast bounded on into Leather Goods. The smells here were confusing, so he had to check out most of the bags. He got his head in a hold-all, and had to shake it off. The hiker's

PVC extra-large rucksack was tough to get open, but he had to get it open in case maybe all twelve of those cats were hiding inside it. But the rucksack was only stuffed with newspaper. The paper got stuck in his teeth, and Blast kept shaking his jowls to try and clear it.

Jim arrived. Shouted, 'Blast, sit! Bad dog.'

Blast glanced at Jim with his puzzled look. Then set off again.

Maybe what he was doing wasn't good. Maybe all these people were getting cross with him. He wasn't hanging around to catch the flack. He needed to catch the cats before Jim caught him.

Blast blasted into the Toy department.

There was a cat flying

round on a piece of string up
near the ceiling. Blast jumped
up four or five times to try and
snap it, but he couldn't reach.

But he did see this cat had wings not whiskers,
so he left it.

The teddy bears nearly fooled him too. But
when he got up close, and sniffed with his
nose, one fell over. And when it fell over, it
made a silly gurgling noise. And Blast knew
straight away that it wasn't a cat.

Then he heard a miaow.

He froze.

His head darted this way and that.

He sniffed.

He smelled no cats.

Then the miaow again.

Blast followed the sound.

There it was, walking towards him.

It was a strange colour for a cat – bright orange. But it had whiskers, and it walked. It walked one stiff leg after the other, with a whirring noise for each step. It went whirr, whirr, whirr, miaow. Whirr, whirr, whirr, miaow.

Blast stared. He was fixed to the spot. This orange striped cat, he didn't even have to chase it. It was coming to him.

One more miaow, and it'd be there with him.

What was he going to do?

Whirr,
whirr, whirr,
miaow.

Blast shuffled backwards.

And then the cat did a strange thing. It stopped walking, and it clicked, and it did a somersault. A back somersault. Blast watched the cat somersault all the way over, and back on to its feet.

The cat whirred off in a different direction. Blast shook his head. Creepy! Not cat. Metal.

'Blast, bad dog sit!'

No way.

Blast put his head down and ran. His head was down, and his ears. All guilty. Pretending he hadn't heard Jim.

A little boy asked Jim, 'Is that your dog?'

'Sort of,' said Jim. 'I'm looking after him.'

'Well,' said the boy, 'you're not having much luck, are you?'

Jim chased off after Blast.

He couldn't find him.

He tried Menswear, Sports Goods, Carpets, Kitchens and Soft Furnishings. There was a rug with toothmarks in Carpets, and a cushion with its stuffing hanging out in Soft Furnishings, but no sign of Blast.

By the main entrance, the store manager was talking to the store detective.

'The dog is obviously mad,' said the manager.

'Yes,' agreed the detective, 'I think we ought to shoot it.'

'Are we allowed to?' asked the manager.

'Well,' said the detective, 'farmers shoot dogs which worry sheep.'

'You can't shoot him,' said Jim.

The manager and the detective turned on him.

'What's it got to do with you?' the manager asked.

'Is he your dog?' the detective added.

'No,' said Jim, 'but I'm looking after him.'

'Well,' said the detective, 'you're not doing a very good job.'

A woman in a smart red uniform came tripping over the carpet. 'I've found him,' she said.

'Where?'

'In Electrical.'

'What's he doing?'

'Watching television.'

The woman led the way, and the manager and the detective followed her, and Jim came along behind.

Sure enough, in Electrical, there was Blast. Sitting patiently in front of a bank of twelve

TV sets, glancing from screen to screen, waiting.

'I'll get my hunting rifle,' said the detective.

'No,' said Jim, 'I'll take care of this.'

This time, he didn't shout at Blast. He strolled over towards him, casually, with his hands in his pockets. Blast glanced up towards him, but then looked back to the TV sets.

Jim sat down on the floor next to Blast.

'What are you watching?' he asked.

Blast glanced at him, and then looked back to the sets.

'Are you waiting for cats?'

Without looking away from the sets, Blast let out a choking kind of sob.

'The thing is,' Jim said, 'they aren't real.'

Blast glanced at him, then back to the TV sets.

'They aren't real, because they're on TV,' Jim went on. 'They're just pictures. If you want to find a real cat, the only place is outside, on the street.'

Jim got up.

Blast looked up at him, then back to the TV sets, then back to Jim again.

Jim said, 'It's up to you. Are you coming or not?'

Blast glanced one more time at the TV sets, then got up. Jim took hold of the lead. As they walked out of the Electrical department, the detective said, 'I'm glad I'm not a cat.'

10. What do I do?

They got to within a few hundred metres of the school. Jim was just preparing what to say to Mrs Andrews, when the next cat happened.

It came out of some bushes in someone's front garden.

It took one look at Blast and hissed back into the bushes and out the other side.

Blast charged through the nearest bush, taking half of it with him.

The cat dodged to the left, to the right, down the passageway between two houses.

The gate at the end of the passageway was shut. There were no gaps, either top or bottom.

The cat ran into a doorway halfway down one side.

Blast bounded past the doorway, stopped with a skid, and turned.

There was the cat.

'Leave it!' Jim shouted.

The cat crouched, all the hair sticking up on its back. It hissed at Blast.

Blast stared at the cat. He looked puzzled.

He was panting. He glanced back at Jim: what do I do now?

A woman leaned out of her window and shouted, 'That horrible brute, he's going to eat my tabby!'

Blast slowly stretched his neck so his nose sniffed towards the cat.

The cat watched the nose. The cat's eyes were wide.

When the nose got to a few centimetres away, the cat struck out with a lightning paw and claw. The claw caught Blast on the nose. He let out a grunt, and stopped sniffing towards the cat. Instead, he tried to see his own nose, if there was any damage.

The cat relaxed. It got up slowly, and licked its armpit casually a couple of times, and then strolled away, as if Blast didn't even exist.

Blast stopped trying to see down his own nose, and watched the cat go. He looked even more puzzled than ever. His face was all wrinkled up in a frown.

Blast watched Jim reach down for the lead. He didn't make any fuss.

When Jim had the lead firmly, he said, 'Come on, then.'

Blast trudged along beside him.

Near the end of the passageway, they passed the cat. The cat was washing itself carefully, slowly, all over. It glanced at Blast. Blast turned his head and stared at the cat. Then grunted, and trudged on.

'That's not a terrier,' said Sarah.

'That's not wire-haired,' said Anna.

'It's a monster,' said Jane.

'He may be a monster,' said Jim, 'but at least he's a dog.'

He led Blast towards the red and white striped tent.

Mrs Andrews stood at a desk by the entrance.

She found Jim's entry card.

Mrs Andrews read the card, then stared at Blast.

'I think there's been a mistake,' she said.

'Bucket is my other dog,' Jim said. 'But he's sick, so I had to bring Blast.'

Mrs Andrews frowned, then crossed

something out on the entry card.

'We'll put him in the large miscellaneous class,' she said. Then pulled back the tent flap.

'This is the grooming area,' she added. 'Where you get ready for the show. When it's your turn, your class gets called and you go through and out into the display arena.'

She gave Jim a ticket.

'Your enclosure is right over there.' She pointed deep into the tent.

Jim led Blast into the big red-and-white-striped tent.

Inside, it was gloomy. The air was thick with doggy smells and doggy howls and whines.

To get to large miscellaneous, they had to pass the small dogs (pedigree), small dogs (sundry), the medium dogs, and the large dogs.

The first dog they passed was Mr Bennett's miniature spaniel.

Mr Bennett was kneeling over the tiny dog, dressing its curls with ribbons.

'Mr Bennett's our maths teacher,' Jim told Blast.

Blast didn't say anything.

But, as soon as Mr Bennett's spaniel saw Blast, it went mad, yapping and snapping and jumping backwards and forwards.

Mr Bennett turned his head. When he saw Blast his eyes went wide.

'What on earth's that?' he said.

'My dog,' replied Jim.

One by one, along the line, alerted by Mr Bennett's spaniel, the other dogs began to yap and snap. As the dogs got bigger, the yapping

got deeper and louder, and the snapping got more fierce.

Jim held the lead tight, and kept on walking.

Blast took no notice of the other dogs. He kept his eyes fixed on the ground just in front of him. Except once or twice he glanced up apologetically. Kept trudging along.

By the time they reached their enclosure, the noise was deafening. All round Blast dogs of all shapes and sizes were howling and yelping and straining at their leads to get at him.

Mrs Andrews came into the tent.

'What's going on?' she demanded.

Mr Bennett clung on to his spaniel's lead with one hand, while pointing at Blast with the other. 'It's that brute over there. He's causing all the trouble.'

'Maybe it's best if we keep him separate,' said Mrs Andrews. And she led Jim and Blast through a side flap in a small, deserted area of the tent.

Immediately, the yapping and snapping and howling died away.

'This is really the First Aid area,' said Mrs Andrews, 'but I'm sure you'll be OK.'

Blast looked up at Jim, then flopped down with a sigh.

12. Judging

The First Aid area had its own hooked-back entrance, so Jim and Blast could see out of the tent.

Outside, people were gathered on the grass in a crowd.

Judges were handing out prizes for earlier categories. Rabbits. Hamsters. Birds. Mice. Each proud winner marched up, clutching their pet, and marched away clutching the pet and a rosette. Blast didn't take much notice.

Then came the cat section.

Jim tensed up. He tightened his grip on the lead.

He tried to get in front of Blast, so the dog couldn't see what was going on.

'Best pedigree, Sarah Williams and Fluffy,'

announced the announcer.

Blast shifted his head this way and that way, trying to see what was going on. Jim moved himself this way and that way, so he got in the way. Sarah got her rosette, and stuck her tongue out at Jim.

Blast let out a shuddering sigh, and looked the other way. The last cat was being brought forward.

'And ugliest moggy, goes to Neil Samuels, with Lucky.'

Blast showed no interest.

Jim breathed a sigh of relief.

Then the judges came, to judge Blast.

'To avoid trouble,' said the woman judge, 'we've decided to do it in here.'

'Away from the other dogs,' said the man judge.

Blast sat like a choirboy. Straight back. Big innocent eyes. He looked like a bouncer outside a nightclub.

'You see,' said Jim, 'it's not his fault, it's all the others try and pick a fight with him.'

'Yes,' said the woman judge, 'he does seem very docile.'

The man judge poked at Blast's fur with his finger. 'Hmmmm,' he said, and frowned.

The woman judge peered closer. 'What's this?'

The man judge peered closer, too. He tutted. The woman shook her head.

Blast glanced down at the spot on his

shoulder where they were prodding.

'What's wrong?' Jim asked.

'I know this is meant to be a fun show,' the woman judge said, 'but some things can't be ignored.'

The man judge stared Jim in the eye. 'This dog has been mistreated,' he said.

'Beaten,' said the woman judge.

'Hit with a stick.'

Jim's throat went tight.

They brought Mrs Andrews in, and Mr Bennett, and they asked Jim questions. Lots of questions. How long he'd had Blast; what he'd done to him.

Blast sat in the corner of the room, watching. Puzzled.

Outside, parents and children and pets waited to see what was going to happen. Jim could hear them murmuring and gossipping.

'He found that dog!'

'He stole it!'

'He beat it!'

Jim had a sore lump tight in his throat. He knew he was going to cry.

'I didn't do anything to him. I wanted to help him and look after him.'

'Then why didn't you take him to the dogs' home, or the police station?'

'What you did is tantamount to theft.'

Mrs Andrews asked, 'Will there be charges?'

'I sincerely hope so,' said the man judge.

'We've contacted the police,' said Mr Bennett.

The sore lump in Jim's throat got bigger.

The woman judge said, 'Some people don't deserve to have pets.'

'RAAAAAAWF!' barked Blast, glaring at the judges from under his eyebrows.

'Ah,' said a voice, 'so that's where he is.'

13. The lipstick woman

A large woman pushed in through the flap of the tent. Her cheeks were swollen like a balloon. She wore high shoes and a short dress. She carried a stick.

'They told me at the police station I might find him here.'

Hearing the voice, Blast flinched, and lowered his head.

The woman stepped briskly up to the judges. Blast's head sank lower.

'I left him for a moment outside a shop, and he must have tugged his lead free,' she said. Her voice was high and fruity.

'Who found him?' she demanded.

'Me,' croaked Jim.

'Thank you so much!' exclaimed the woman, and leaned down and kissed him on the cheek. Her lips were slimy with gloss.

Jim rubbed at the mark they left.

'Don't I know you?' the woman judge asked.

The lipstick woman shook her head. 'I hardly think so.'

'Is this your dog?' the man judge asked.

'Yes,' said the woman.

'He's been beaten,' the woman judge said.

The woman's small eyes widened. She looked from judge, to judge, to Blast, to Jim.

'You vile child!' she exclaimed. 'You cruel and nasty piece of work.'

And she raised her hand, as if she was going to slap Jim.

'RAAAAWF!'

Blast flung himself, and barged the woman so she sat PLONK on her backside. Then, he was away.

Blast flew out of the tent, out into the crowds of people and pets. Cats yowled, dogs barked, a parrot squawked. Blast took no notice. Head down, he ran.

'Stop him!' howled the lipstick woman.

'Watch out!' shouted Mrs Andrews.

'Blast!' shouted Jim, and chased after the dog.

Blast bounded on, through the crowd, towards the gates, past the ornamental pond with fountains.

By the ornamental pond a small girl was

sailing her small boat. She looked up, saw Blast, stepped back. Into the water.

'Help!' shouted the mother.

'Help!' gurgled the child, splashing and crying. Blast bounded on two bounds, then skidded to a halt, and swung round. He bounded over the small wall, and into the pond. Jim tried to jump the wall from the other side, but caught his toe, and went head first into the water. Jim coughed and choked and splashed with his arms.

When he surfaced, everyone was racing towards the pool.

Mr Bennett was shouting, 'Oh my goodness, the brute's going to eat her!'

Blast was swimming with his head up, paws going like paddles. Towards the little girl.

'Help!' she gurgled.

'RAAAAWF!' Blast barked. And lunged his head towards her, with his mouth wide open.

'No!' shouted the girl's mother.

Blast's head plunged underwater, like a shark going in for the kill.

When his head reappeared, his mouth was closed on something. He was swimming furiously. His head was high.

Then the lipstick woman arrived. One of her shoes was broken, so she had to hobble. She was waving the stick.

'He's always been a bad, bad, bad, disobedient animal,' she puffed.

Blast hauled himself out of the pool. In his mouth he had a mouthful of the girl's T-shirt. The girl was still inside the T-shirt. Blast laid her carefully on the ground, then shook himself so the water flew off in jewels.

'Bad dog! Leave her alone!' shouted the woman, hobbling round the side of the pond, waving her stick.

'Leave him alone!' shouted Jim, and floundered over, and grabbed at the woman's arm.

'He saved her!' shouted the girl's mother.

'Yes,' said the man judge, 'he kept her head

above the water.'

But the lipstick woman pulled her arm free, and raised her stick high above her head.

'No!' shouted Jim.

'It's the only language he understands,' she said, pushing Jim away.

'No it's not!' said Jim. But the woman was too strong for him.

Blast looked up, saw the stick, and as it swished down, slithered to his feet and ran.

The stick cracked on the concrete, and snapped.

'Always causing trouble!' snarled the lipstick woman, and turned on Jim, 'and you're no better.'

'Now I remember!' said the woman judge, pushing herself between the lipstick woman and Jim.

'Don't touch him,' added the man judge. The lipstick woman lowered her hand, shrank back.

'You can't prove anything.'

'Last year, five charges of cruelty to animals?'

'We've got some questions to ask you,' said the woman judge to the lipstick woman.

'Not now,' said the lipstick woman. Turning away. But as she turned, she overbalanced on the broken shoe, and tumbled, helpless, into the pond.

Jim didn't stop to look. He chased off after Blast.

But he ran straight into the arms of his mum.

14. My dog

Jim and his mum sat up late in the kitchen, talking.

'That's why I wanted to go to the show,' Jim's mum told him, 'to have a look at the pets.'

'Why?'

'To see whether maybe we could have a dog sort of thing after all.'

Jim fiddled with his cereal bowl.

'I don't want a dog. I want Blast.'

'What's so special about Blast?'

'You'd know, if you saw him.'

'He belongs to that lady.'

'You heard what the judge man said. She's horrible. She runs a breeding farm and she's cruel and she beats the dogs, and keeps dead puppies in the fridge and she pretends she's all nice and she sells them to nasty people for experiments.'

'Well, anyway,' Jim's mum said, 'he's run away.'

'I'm going out to look for him tomorrow.'

'OK,' said Jim's mum. 'I'll come and help.'

That night, Jim couldn't sleep. Every time he shut his eyes he saw dogs, and large women beating them, and the judges were chasing him with their clipboards.

Around ten, he got out of bed. He had this feeling.

He opened the curtains. There, in the moonlight, sitting patiently in the middle of the garden, was a fat, scary-looking dog.

In the morning, when Jim's mum came into his bedroom, she gasped, 'What on earth is that?'

Blast stretched, and yawned. The bed creaked.

'My dog,' Jim said.

If you enjoyed *Is That Your Dog?* you might like these stories, too.

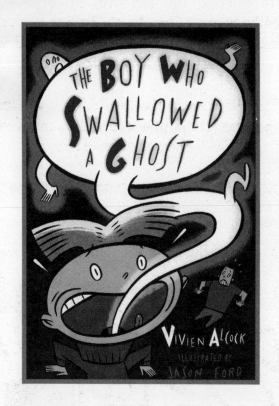

THE BOY WHO
SWALLOWED A GHOST
BY VIVIEN ALCOCK

If the school champion turned to you for help, would you refuse?

Mike is out of his depth. Prince – everyone's hero – is terrified about something, and he's turned to Mike for help.

Prince's story is too incredible to be true, yet his fear is real enough, and this is Mike's chance to save his idol.

But how can Mike help if he doesn't even believe?

Hurricane Summer

by Robert Swindells

It's World War II and Jim has a fantastic new
friend – a fighter pilot.

Jim worships Cocky and looks forward
to his every visit.

But war has a way of changing people's lives –
and friendships may bring pain as well as joy.

By the winner of the Carnegie Medal